19.95

SAMURAI WARRIORS

by Lois Sepahban

Published by The Child's World
1980 Lookout Drive • Mankato, MN 56003-1705
800-599-READ • www.childsworld.com

ACKNOWLEDGMENTS
The Child's World®: Mary Berendes, Publishing Director
Red Line Editorial: Editorial direction
The Design Lab: Design
Amnet: Production
Content Consultant: Dr. Stephen Turnbull, Visiting Professor
of Japanese Studies, Akita International University, Japan
Design elements: iStockphoto
Photographs ©: The Print Collector/Corbis, cover; Asian Art
& Archaeology, Inc./Corbis, 4, 22; Hayashi Masaki/Shutter-
stock Images, 6; Library of Congress, 10, 30 (bottom);
Burstein Collection/Corbis, 11; Shutterstock Images, 12, 16,
30 (top); 68/Ocean/Corbis, 14; Alex Milan Tracy/Demotix/
Corbis, 15; Maxim Tupikov/Shutterstock Images, 20–21;
Toyokuni Utagawa, 23; Utagawa Kuniyoshi, 24; Keren Su/
Corbis, 26, 30 (middle); Public Domain, 27, 28

ISBN 9781631437595
LCCN 2014945423

Printed in the United States of America
Mankato, MN
November, 2014
PA02246

ABOUT THE AUTHOR

Lois Sepahban has written several science, history, biography, and fiction books for children. She lives in Kentucky with her husband and two children.

TABLE OF CONTENTS

Yoritomo Minamoto became the first shogun of Japan.

CHAPTER ONE

THE SAMURAI CODE

Emperors once ruled Japan's empire. But from 1192 to 1868, war leaders called shoguns were the most powerful rulers of the country. In 1600, samurai families fought to choose the next shogun. Some samurai families wanted the shogun to be Mitsunari Ishida. Other samurai families wanted the shogun to be Ieyasu Tokugawa.

Mototada Torii was Tokugawa's general. He kept Fushimi Castle safe for Tokugawa. He had an army of approximately 2,000 samurai warriors.

Torii knew that his small army could not keep Fushimi Castle safe from Ishida's much larger army.

Fushimi Castle is near Kyoto, Japan.

He also knew that Tokugawa needed time to gather more warriors to fight Ishida.

For 11 days, Torii and his warriors fought Ishida's army. When he had only a few warriors left, Torii knew that Ishida's army would finally get inside the castle. Because he didn't want to be captured alive, Torii killed himself.

Torii became an example of the samurai code of honor. He was loyal to his lord, Tokugawa. He did not run away from a battle. He fought bravely and with **dignity**.

Because the army was slowed down for 11 days, Tokugawa was able to gather more warriors. Later that year, Ishida was defeated in battle by Tokugawa. The new shogun's family ruled Japan for more than 200 years.

The Way Of The Warrior

The samurai code was called *bushido*, or the way of the warrior. It was based on honor, **discipline**, and moral values. A samurai warrior had to be willing to die for his lord. The code reminded samurai warriors that they could die at any moment. To be ready to die, they had to bathe every day. Their clothing and armor had to be clean. They learned to act correctly at their time of death as well. Dying calmly and with dignity was important. *Bushido* also reminded samurai warriors that they belonged to a special group. Not just anyone could become a samurai warrior.

Another View
WITHOUT A LORD

A samurai warrior fought for his lord. If a samurai warrior's lord was defeated or died, the samurai became *ronin*. That meant he was a samurai warrior with no lord. Often, *ronin* would find a new lord to fight for. But sometimes, he could not. The samurai code stated that a samurai warrior must serve a lord. Being *ronin* was shameful. How do you think samurai felt about becoming *ronin*?

CHAPTER TWO

THE RISE OF THE SAMURAI

In 1100, Japan's emperor lived in the city of Kyoto. At that time, Japan was made up of **provinces**. Many provinces were far away from Kyoto. It was difficult for the emperor to travel to the provinces and govern the people there. So the emperor employed government officials in the provinces to watch over the country's people. Some of the officials were the emperor's sons. When they left Kyoto, the emperor's sons took new last names. Some took the family names of Minamoto and Taira. These two families grew to be very powerful.

The Minamoto and Taira families worked with the *bushidan* in in the provinces. The *bushidan* were groups of warriors. They followed a chieftain or lord.

These chieftains were landowners. They needed warriors to protect their lands. The warriors promised to fight for their lord. They promised to be loyal to him and obey him. In return, the lord promised to protect his followers. Over time, the *bushidan* became the warrior class called the samurai.

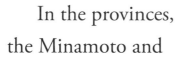

Samurai were fierce warriors.

In the provinces, the Minamoto and Taira families became the leaders of the samurai. The families grew wealthy and powerful. But from 1160 to 1185, the Taira and Minamoto families fought for power. Each family wanted to be the most powerful. The Minamoto won. In 1192, the Minamoto family set up the first warrior government in Japan.

Their leader was Yoritomo Minamoto. Because he controlled a large army, he was more powerful than the emperor. The emperor gave him the title *Seii Taishogun,* which means a general who conquers barbarians. This made him the first shogun in Japan.

For nearly 700 years, shoguns ruled Japan. During that time, Japan still had emperors, but they did not have as much power as the shoguns.

Serving the shogun were samurai warriors. The samurai did not have the highest rank in Japan.

The Taira warriors were always ready to fight.

The shogun ruled Japan from Kyoto.

The highest rank belonged to the emperor and noble families. But the samurai did have power. *Daimyo* were powerful samurai warriors. They owned large estates and castles. They used their power to help shoguns rule Japan for centuries.

Geography of Japan

Japan has four main islands. Hokkaido is the farthest north. Honshu is south of Hokkaido. It is the largest island with both Kyoto and Edo (modern-day Tokyo). Shikoku is south of Honshu. And Kyushu is the most western island. There are also many smaller islands. Volcanoes created the islands of Japan. The steep mountains made travel and communication difficult. Governing each region was challenging for a ruler based in Kyoto.

Another View
Samurai Women

While samurai warriors were away from home fighting wars, their wives were in charge. A samurai wife ran the household. She cared for her children. She learned to fight with a dagger or knife in case her home was invaded. Yet a samurai woman had to obey her father when she was young. She obeyed her husband when married. And she obeyed her son when she became a widow. Do you think it was harder to be a woman or a man in a samurai family? Why or why not?

CHAPTER THREE

UNIFORMS AND WEAPONS

Before 1600, samurai warriors used two main weapons: swords and bows and arrows. The sword was the samurai's favorite weapon. Only the samurai were allowed to carry two swords. The samurai code stated that a warrior must carry his sword wherever he went.

Samurai warriors learned *kendo*, which is the art of sword fighting. They usually wore two swords: one long and one short sword. The long sword was the main

Swords were samurai's most valued weapons.

A samurai's armor helped protect warriors and scare their enemies.

Samurai fighting armor was finely crafted.

fighting sword. Some samurai fought with both swords, one in each hand. These swords were practical in battle. They were also a symbol of the samurai.

Along with his swords, a samurai prized his armor. In battle, armor protected the warrior from an enemy's weapons. The *cuirass* was made of iron panels held together with leather or silk straps. It protected a samurai's chest, sides, and back. The iron panels sometimes had chain mail to make them stronger. Special plates covered the arms and shins.

A helmet was made of several iron plates joined together. A wooden crest sat on the top of the helmet. The crest curved upward like horns. Metal masks could also be worn to protect the face. These masks were often painted rcd to appear more frightening in battle.

Samurai Training

To become a samurai, a male child had to be born or adopted into a samurai family. Samurai boys started school at age seven. Boys might learn at home, or they might be sent to live with their teacher. Teachers were often male relatives. The students learned battle skills. They listened to war stories. They learned discipline and respect. Their training included sword fighting, archery, and hunting with dogs while on horseback.

Another View
Zen Buddhism

Buddhism is a religion that started in Asia. The form of Buddhism that was more popular in Japan was called Zen.

Meditation is an important part of Zen Buddhism. Samurai practiced Zen Buddhism. They believed that meditation helped them become better warriors. But Buddhists do not believe in killing. Do you think it was easy for a samurai warrior to follow Zen Buddhism? Why or why not?

CHAPTER FOUR

BATTLE TACTICS

Discipline was important in the samurai army.
A disciplined warrior acted bravely. He obeyed orders.
He did not run away from battle. A samurai warrior
wanted his mind to be calm when he died. He didn't
want to be afraid. The samurai code taught warriors to
face their deaths with courage.

Most samurai battles were surprise attacks. Samurai
warriors set fire to the buildings in a village. When they
attacked a castle, they tried to set fire to three sides of it.
They killed everyone who tried to escape: men, women,
and children.

Away from villages, samurai armies fought on
battlefields. Samurai warriors fought on horseback and
followed their leader's orders. Tokugawa was known

Samurai were skilled at fighting in battles.

for telling his warriors that there were only two ways to return from battle. They could return with their enemy's head or without their own. Giving up was not an option.

If a *daimyo* was defeated in battle, he was sometimes allowed to promise his loyalty to the

victor. If he was willing to do this, he could return to his lands. But the samurai code said that this was shameful. So instead, many defeated samurai leaders used their short swords to kill themselves. This ritual is called *seppuku*. The samurai warrior would cut open his own belly. He preferred to die than to live with shame.

Samurai Shigetada Hatakeyama leaves the
battlefield bloodied and wounded.

ARCHERY DUEL

Battles between samurai armies began with an archery **duel**. In an archery duel, a samurai warrior shouted his name to the enemy warriors. He also shouted his achievements in other battles. On the other side, a samurai warrior shouted back. Then the two warriors raced their horses toward each other. They shot arrows at each other. Then they fought on foot using swords or daggers. The winner cut off the loser's head. Then he rode back to his army with the head.

Samurai shot arrows during duels.

ANOTHER VIEW
OTHER SOLDIERS

Not all soldiers in a samurai army were samurai warriors. Some, called *ashigaru*, were not born into samurai families. They could not carry the two samurai swords. Instead, they fought with a lance, or a long pole with a sharp point. The *ashigaru* fought on foot instead of on horseback. They also did not have to follow the samurai code. Do you think battle was easier for *ashigaru* or samurai? Why?

Ashigaru used firearms in battle after the weapons were brought to Japan.

CHAPTER FIVE

SAMURAI IN BATTLE

In 1281, the emperor of China wanted to invade Japan. This emperor was Kublai Khan. He wanted to conquer all of Asia. Seven years earlier, he had tried to invade Japan. But almost all of his ships were destroyed in a storm.

The people of Japan were afraid of Kublai Khan's soldiers. The khan was a Mongol. Mongols were known as brutal fighters. To protect Japan from the khan, the shogun had a wall built along the western coast of the island of Kyushu. This would be the first place Kublai Khan's army would try to invade.

Kublai Khan was a powerful leader of China during the 13th century.

Samurai warriors defended the wall from
Kublai Khan and the Chinese warriors.

In 1281, the Chinese army came with more than
4,000 ships and 140,000 soldiers. They landed in
Hakata on Kyushu. When the Chinese army arrived,
messages were sent across Japan. The samurai of
Kyushu needed more warriors. But it would take weeks
for more warriors to arrive. If the Chinese army got
past the walls at Hakata, nothing could stop them from
taking over the island.

Samurai warriors boarded the Chinese ships,
attacking the invaders.

For several weeks, the samurai warriors fought the
Chinese army. The samurai did not let the Chinese
soldiers break the wall. The Chinese army thought the
warriors of Japan would be easy to defeat. They were
wrong. After a storm destroyed most of their ships, the
Chinese army left Japan.

The warriors of Hakata were samurai. They
followed the samurai code. They did not run away
from battle. They fought bravely and they faced death
with courage.

Kusunoki

In 1331, the Hojo army captured Emperor Go-Daigo during a battle. The Hojos were a ruling shogun family. A samurai warrior named Kusunoki fought for the emperor in the battle. He escaped capture, but the Hojos sent the emperor and his family to a small island. Kusunoki continued to fight for the emperor. He and his samurai warriors captured an important castle. They fought off the large Hojo army in a famous battle. The emperor was then able to escape and regain control from the Hojos.

Another View
WESTERN TRADERS

The first westerners to arrive in Japan were Portuguese traders. They arrived in 1543. Samurai guards spotted the large ships off the coast of the island of Tanegashima. Their *daimyo* welcomed the westerners. He watched as Portuguese traders shot a duck into the air with a firearm called a *harquebus*. The *daimyo* purchased two of the new weapons. Within a few years, the *harquebus* was being made in Japan. Firearms replaced bows and arrows in battles. How do you think western traders affected the samurai?

TIMELINE

1100
Japan's emperor employs officials to run provinces of Japan.

1192
The Minamoto family sets up the first warrior government in Japan.

1281
The emperor of China attempts to invade Japan. Japan wins the battle.

1331
Emperor Go-Daigo is captured by the Hojo army during a battle.

1543
The Portuguese land in Japan. They introduce firearms to the Japanese people.

1600
Ieyasu Tokugawa becomes the shogun.

1868
Shoguns and samurai lose control of the Japanese empire.

GLOSSARY

Buddhism (BOO-diz-uhm) Buddhism is a religion that is based on the teachings of Buddha. Some samurai warriors followed Zen Buddhism.

dignity (DIG-nuh-tee) A person with dignity has qualities that make others respect or honor that person. It was important for samurai to die with dignity.

discipline (DISS-uh-plin) To have discipline is to have control over the way you or others behave. Discipline was an important part of the samurai code.

duel (DOO-uhl) A duel is a fight between two people that has strict rules about the method of fighting. Samurai battles started with a duel.

emperors (EM-pur-orz) Emperors are the male rulers of a society. Shoguns had more power than emperors.

meditation (med-i-TAY-shun) Meditation is a mental exercise that calms and relaxes the mind and body. Samurai believed meditation helped them become better warriors.

provinces (PROV-uhnss-sez) Provinces are sections of a country. It was difficult for the emperor to rule the provinces of Japan.

victor (VIK-tur) A victor is the winner of a battle or contest. A defeated *daimyo* could promise his loyalty to the victor of a battle.

TO LEARN MORE

BOOKS

Macdonald, Fiona. *A Samurai Warrior.*
Mankato, MN: Book House, 2015.

Turnbull, Stephen R. *The Samurai Capture a King: Okinawa,
1609.* Oxford, UK: Osprey Publishing, 2009.

WEB SITES

Visit our Web site for links about samurai warriors:
childsworld.com/links

Note to Parents, Teachers, and Librarians: We routinely verify our Web links to make
sure they are safe and active sites. So encourage your readers to check them out!

INDEX